D1326017

First published in Great Britain in 2009
by Hodder Children's Books

1

A Catalogue record for this book is available
from the British Library

ISBN 978 0 340 98147 4 (HB)
ISBN 978 0 340 98153 5 (PB)

Typeset by Tony Fleetwood

Printed and bound in Great Britain by
Clays Ltd, St Ives plc, Bungay, Suffolk
The paper used in this book is a natural recyclable product made from
wood grown in sustainable forests. The hard coverboard is recycled.

Hodder Children's Books
a division of Hachette Children's Books
338 Euston Road, London NW1 3BH
An Hachette UK company
www.hachette.co.uk

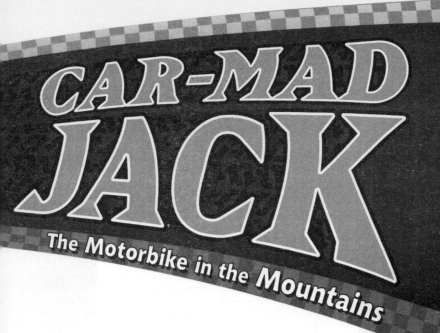

CAR-MAD JACK
The Motorbike in the Mountains

Written by
JENNY ALEXANDER

Illustrated by
MARK OLIVER

Hodder
Children's
Books

A division of Hachette Children's Books

· CHAPTER 1 ·

It had been a horrible week.

On Monday, Jack came bottom in his times-tables test.

On Tuesday, his grumpy big sister got into a grump that lasted for three whole days.

On Wednesday, his baby brother started potty-training.

On Thursday, his mum got stressed from cleaning up puddles and poos.

On Friday, Miss Sims kept him in at

playtime for drawing cars instead of learning his times-tables.

Jack couldn't wait for Saturday to come. 'A whole morning at the car supermarket with Dad,' he thought. 'Nothing can spoil that.'

But there was one thing that could spoil it – Jack's nasty cousin, Clark. He didn't come to the car supermarket every week. He only came if Dad and Uncle Archie had some jobs for him. He didn't really like cars at all. He just liked the extra pocket money.

'Guess what?' said Dad, when Mum dropped Jack off at the car supermarket at the end of his horrible week. 'Clark might be coming in later. Won't that be nice?'

Jack's heart sank into his boots.

'As nice as swimming with crocodiles,' he thought.

But he didn't have time to worry about it because Dad wanted to show him something. He seemed very excited. He strode out of the showroom with Jack at his heels.

'We've never had one of these before,' he said. 'Just wait until you see it, Jack!

You're going to love it!'

Jack tried to think what kind of car they had never had in the car supermarket before – a Rolls Royce, a Lotus, a Lamborghini? But then he saw it! It wasn't a car at all. It was a motorbike.

'It's a Triumph Bonneville,' said Dad. 'Made in Britain. What do you think?'

The sun danced on the gleaming silver engine with all its pipes and spirals. It shone on the bright blue tank and the leather seat. It lit up the silver spokes of the wheels and sparkled on the handlebars. Jack was dazzled.

'It's beautiful,' he said.

'A work of art,' agreed Dad.

They gazed at it in silence for a few minutes. Then Dad said, 'My father had

one of these when I was a boy.'

Jack was astonished.

'What ... Grandpa?' he gasped. Jack's
Grandpa worked in the bank. He had
short white hair and wore a suit. It was
impossible to imagine him in a helmet
and leather jacket, sitting on a big shiny
motorbike.

Dad laughed.

'Grandpa didn't always work in the bank

and drive a BMW,' he said. 'When he was younger he was motorbike-mad. He loved his Bonneville. He said it was a beefy bike – big and powerful like a prize bull.'

Dad put his hands on the handlebars as if he was going to get on. 'If I had one of these, I'd go on a road trip. I'd ride it right up through England and Scotland, all the way to the top.'

Dad said the North of Scotland was perfect touring country. It was a land of high mountains and rocky rivers and sandy beaches. The roads were empty up there. You could ride all day and hardly meet another person.

'It would be a real adventure,' Dad said.
'You would be all on your own in a wild
lonely place, and anything could happen.
You could hit bad weather, like gale-force
winds that would make it hard to keep
the bike on the road. You could get lost.
You could break down or run out of petrol,

miles from anywhere.'

Dad said you would have to take emergency supplies, like a tent and a torch and some food. Jack wondered if he would be brave enough to go on an adventure like that. He asked if he could sit on the beefy Bonneville. Dad let go of the handles and stood back. He scratched his chin. 'I don't know ...' he said.

'Please?' said Jack. 'I'll be careful. I won't mess around.'

Dad said Jack could sit on the bike as long as he was there. He held it while Jack climbed on, but he didn't really need to because the centre stand held the bike steady. The curved leather seat was soft and wide, higher at the back where a passenger could sit.

Just then, Mrs Merridew came out of the office with a pile of letters in her hands.

'I need you to sign these before I put them in the post,' she said to Dad.

He hesitated.

'The post goes in five minutes,' Mrs Merridew added.

Dad looked at Jack.

'I'll be OK,' Jack said. 'You go in and sign the letters.'

He watched Dad disappear into the office with Mrs Merridew.

'It's just you and me now,' he said softly to the motorbike. 'Just you and me and the open road.'

He had to lean right forward to reach the handlebars. The grips were thick and wide. There were switches beside his hands, and two big dials that looked up like eyes from the middle of the handlebars, with the windscreen in front of them.

Jack didn't want to waste time driving all the way through England on the motorways. He just wanted to be in Scotland among the mountains. He shut

his eyes – and he was there. He could smell
the mountain air. He could feel the wind
on his face.

In real life, driving from the car
supermarket to the North of Scotland
would take all day and most of the night.
Jack knew that because he had been to
Scotland on holiday when he was little,

though he didn't really remember it. But in a pretend game you could be there in seconds.

'Oh bother,' thought Jack. 'I forgot to pack a tent and a torch and some food.'

But it was a lovely sunny day. The mountains looked hazy and blue in the distance. He didn't think the weather would turn bad, and he had plenty of petrol in his tank.

The big engine rumbled, like a wild bull pawing the ground. It wanted to get going.

'Everything will be fine,' thought Jack.

He released the brake and opened the throttle.

· CHAPTER 2 ·

Ro-o-o-o-a-a-r!

The Bonneville belted off down the road.
There was no other traffic in sight, not
a single car, lorry or bike. There were no
buildings or pavements or roundabouts or
traffic lights. There was just the empty road
snaking across the moors towards the far
away mountains.

But the road was narrow, only wide
enough for one car. It had passing places
you could pull into if you met any traffic.

There were deep ditches on both sides. The edges had crumbled away in places and there were lots of potholes. In a car, that wouldn't be too scary. But on a bike it felt really dangerous. If he hit a big pothole, he might lose his balance. He might swerve right off the road and end up in the bog.

There were other dangers too, like the scruffy sheep and shaggy cows dotted about the countryside. There weren't any

fences, so one of them could wander into the road at any moment. Jack slowed down until he felt more in control.

He rode for miles, past little lakes and rocky rivers, and he didn't see anyone else at all. Sometimes he saw buildings, but when he got close he found they were just empty shells with no roof or windows. People had lived here once, but not any more. It was starting to feel a bit eerie.

The road got more winding and steep as Jack rode up into the mountains. The air was colder now, and the mist was coming down.

'It'll be all right,' he thought. 'I can still get past the mountains before night-time.'

But the mist was getting thicker. Soon, Jack could hardly see the road ahead. He turned his headlight on, but it didn't help. He had to slow right down to a crawl. He didn't know where he was any more, or even if he was going in the right direction. He stopped.

Jack took out his mobile phone. He would have to call the police or mountain rescue services. But what would he say? He couldn't tell them where he was and they wouldn't be able to look for him in the

thick mist. Still, he had to try. He switched
on his phone. No signal.

In the swirling mist he could just make
out the dark shape of a building. Maybe it
was a house. Maybe someone was at home.
He stood his motorbike on its stand and
trudged across the wet grass towards the
building.

It was an old stone barn with a tin roof
and a hole in the back wall. Jack pushed

through the broken door. It was dry inside, and he could dimly see some hay and sticks in the corner. He decided to stay there until the mist cleared.

He wished he had brought some food because he felt really hungry. He wished he had a torch too, now that the night was closing in. He shivered. At least he could make a fire. He knew how because he had seen someone on TV doing it, using only a stick, a stone and a bit of hay.

He was too busy to feel scared while he was making his fire. But when he sat back on his heels, he noticed that it had got dark.

Crackle, crackle went the fire in the empty barn.

Ooo went the wind in the mountains.

Huff, huff, snuffle!

Jack froze. There was someone right outside. He could hear them breathing. They were huff, huff, snuffling round the back of the barn.

Jack watched and waited, hardly daring to breathe.

A big hairy nose appeared through the hole in the wall. Then a big hairy face. A Highland cow looked in. She huff, snuffled as she looked at Jack in the flickering firelight. She disappeared back into the darkness, and Jack was on his own again.

Crackle, crackle went the fire in the empty barn.

Ooo went the wind in the mountains.

Cough, cough!

Jack froze. There was someone right outside the door. He heard them coughing.

Cough, cough … thud!

They were pushing against the broken door.

Jack stood up and backed towards the

wall. The door scraped open a little bit.
Then it opened a little bit more.

Cough, shuffle, shove!

A sheep with half its wool hanging off
pushed through the gap and stood there
blinking in the firelight.

Cough!

Jack suddenly remembered someone telling him that a sheep's cough sounded just like a human being's. The startled sheep squeezed back through the broken door and ran away into the night. Jack was on his own again.

Crackle, crackle went the fire in the empty barn.

Ooo went the wind in the mountains.

Then faintly, in the distance, Jack heard a ghostly sound. He listened hard. It sounded like bagpipes – but what was a piper doing, walking around in the mountains on a night like this? A chill of fear went through him like cold water trickling down his back. Could it be Clark McClark, the famous ghost of the glen?

The tinny sound of the bagpipes was

getting clearer. It wasn't bagpipes! It was an MP3 player. Suddenly, the pretend game melted away. Jack was back in the car supermarket. Clark was coming round the corner, fiddling with his MP3 player.

Jack sat very still. Maybe Clark wouldn't notice him. Then he could go back to his adventure in the Highlands of Scotland. If

Clark saw him he would come over and spoil everything, just like he always did.

Mrs Merridew came out, calling for Clark. She had a job for him. Clark didn't like working – he just liked getting paid. So he sloped off towards the workshop before she spotted him.

That was good news for Jack, because now he could get back to his game.

· CHAPTER 3 ·

The mist had cleared. It was a fine sunny morning in the mountains. Jack set off on his motorbike again. He came to a small stone bridge over a rocky river and stopped to drink some water. He felt happy and excited. Soon he would see the sea up ahead. He was nearly there.

For a long time, the engine sounded strong and steady. The Bonneville wasn't a fast racing bike – it was a tourer. It was built for long-distance riding. It took the up-hills in its stride and cruised along on the flat.

But suddenly it started losing speed. The engine spluttered. It cut out altogether. Jack had broken down. He got off the bike. He thought he might have run out of petrol but there was still some petrol in the tank. He checked all the gleaming pipes and spirals. He couldn't see what the problem was.

His mobile phone still had no signal, so

he couldn't call for breakdown recovery. He would have to walk and push his motorbike. But it was very heavy. He knew he wouldn't be able to get very far. He might have to leave the bike and bring a mechanic back here to mend it.

He was standing by the bike deciding what to do when Clark's voice dragged him right back to the car supermarket again.

'Hey, Flapjack! Isn't that motorbike a bit big for a weedy little titch like you?'

'Mrs Merridew's looking for you,' said Jack. 'Dad's looking for you too, and so is Uncle Archie. They've all got jobs for you.'

Clark just laughed and took no notice.

'Well, are you going to try and get on, then?' he mocked. 'Or is it just too big and scary?'

'I've been sitting on it,' Jack told him. 'I've just got off.'

'Fell off, more likely,' said Clark.

He gave Jack a nasty look. Jack knew that look. It was the one that meant he had just had an idea for a mean scheme.

Clark opened his mouth and yelled.

'Help, help! Come quick!' he shouted.

He ran towards the showroom. 'Jack's been

playing on the motorbike – and he's fallen off!'

Dad came running out, with Mrs Merridew close behind.

'Is he all right?' he asked, looking worried. 'I just went in for a few minutes. I forgot he was playing on the bike.'

'I don't know,' Clark said. 'I just saw him

on the ground and came to get help.'

'Well done, Clark,' said Mrs Merridew.
'You did the right thing.'

Mrs Merridew and Dad stood fussing
over Jack. They wanted to know what
happened. How had he fallen off? Had
he hurt himself? If he had been messing
around, then he was lucky the motorbike
hadn't fallen on top of him.

'I'm fine,' he said. 'I didn't fall off.'

They looked at each other. Jack could tell
that they didn't believe him. Dad told Mrs
Merridew to go back inside. 'We'll be all
right now,' he said. Then he turned to Jack.

'Tell me what happened,' he said.

'I was playing, and I got off. It was part
of the game.'

'Hmm,' said Dad. 'Then why did

Clark say you fell off?'

'To get me into trouble and spoil my game,' Jack told him.

'But why would he want to do that?' asked Dad.

Jack shrugged. He had no idea why Clark liked spoiling things – he just did.

'Tell me the truth,' said Dad. 'I won't be angry.'

Jack didn't like telling anyone about his pretend games because that could take away the magic. But this time, he had to. He had to explain why he had got off the motorbike.

'It was part of the story,' he said. 'I was riding through the mountains, like you said. I was going to the top of Britain. The motorbike broke down, so I had to get off and push it.'

Dad nodded as if he could see the mountains too, and the long road and the broken-down motorbike.

'I got off very carefully,' added Jack.

Dad said he was sorry for not believing Jack. He knew that Jack wouldn't mess around and be silly at the car supermarket. He loved the cars too much and his

Saturdays there were important to him.

'I'm going to have a talk with Clark,' he said. 'I can put up with his laziness and bad attitude because Uncle Archie wants us to let him work here. But I won't put up with him making trouble for you.'

Jack thought that Dad would go straight away, but he hung around.

'It sounds like a great game,' he said. 'Are you going to phone for breakdown recovery?'

'No signal,' said Jack.

'You might have a long walk then, unless someone comes by. I suppose you might see some other motorbikes or a passing camper van.'

'I haven't seen anyone else all day,' Jack said. 'Or all night. That was scary.'

'Well here's some advice for you,' said Dad. 'Slap on lots of insect cream. The midges are murder in Scotland at this time of year.'

'Midges?' said Jack.

'They're like tiny mosquitoes. You don't notice them when you're moving, but as soon as you stop, they're all over you. It feels like you're being eaten alive.'

Jack shuddered. He decided the first thing he would do when he went back to his game would be to cover himself from head to toe in insect cream.

'Right. Now where is that nephew of mine?' said Dad, looking around for Clark. 'That boy is never around when you want him.'

· CHAPTER 4 ·

Jack smothered himself in insect cream
— just in time! A black cloud of midges was
coming straight at him. They stopped when
they got near him. They hovered close by,
buzzing and whining. Jack wondered how
the insect cream worked. Did the midges
just hate the smell of it? Or would it zap
them dead if they landed on it?

He went back to pushing the heavy
motorbike. It was easier now because he
was coming down out of the mountains,

but he was very tired. The cloud of midges
followed close behind.

He hadn't gone far when he heard
another sound behind him, above the buzz
and whine of the midges. He stopped to
listen. It was the throb of an engine. As it
came nearer, he realised it was more than
one engine.

Three motorbikes were coming down

the hill. He flagged them down. The riders pulled over and got off their bikes. They seemed very friendly.

'Nice bike,' said one.

'Are you riding alone?' said another.

The third one said, 'Is there a problem?'

Jack explained about his adventure. He told them what had happened with his motorbike.

'Sounds like the transmission,' the biker said.

Jack didn't know what the transmission was – it was just a word he had heard. But the three bikers knew, and they were carrying spare parts. Before long, they had mended it. They asked Jack if he would like to ride with them for the rest of the way.

Jack liked the idea of riding in a pack. He imagined the throb and rumble of all those big engines together. He remembered his scary night in the barn. It would have been much less scary if it would have been with these three friendly bikers. It would be safer riding with them, but it would also be less of an adventure.

So Jack said goodbye and thank you to the three bikers. He watched them go roaring off down the road in a cloud of dust. Then he got back on the beefy

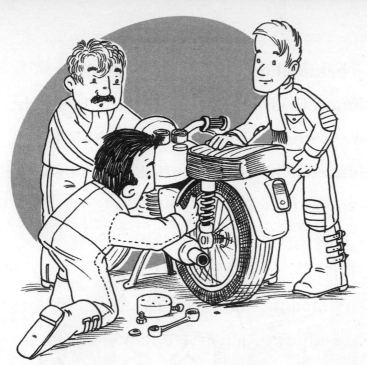

Bonneville and started the engine. He rode
down from the mountains. The countryside
was getting flatter, but he still couldn't see
the sea.

Dad was right. You didn't notice the
midges as long as you kept moving. The
wind in your face blew them away. It felt
good to be back on the road again.

Jack didn't hear the motorbike coming

up behind him until it suddenly drew
alongside his bike. It looked as if he might
have someone to ride with after all. He
glanced across at the other rider. The smile
froze on his face.

It was Clark!

Jack looked away. He hoped Clark
would pull ahead and overtake him. But he

seemed to want to ride side by side.

'Big bike!' Clark yelled above the noise of the engines. 'A bit too big for a weedy little fellow like you!'

Jack tried to ignore him.

'Bet you're scared of falling off!' yelled Clark.

'Go away, go away, go away,' thought Jack. But he didn't say anything.

'You should stick to something smaller,' Clark shouted. 'Something like a push-bike!'

Jack speeded up, but Clark speeded up too. He slowed down again. Clark slowed down too.

'Do I get the feeling you don't want to ride with me?' Clark yelled. He laughed a nasty laugh. 'Well too bad! You're stuck with me! Get over it!'

Jack couldn't shake Clark off. He was like those pesky midges, hovering and whining around him when he had to get off and walk. At least he had lots of insect cream on, so they couldn't land on him.

That thought gave him an idea. He had lots of insect cream on – but what if Clark didn't? Then, if they stopped, the midges would swarm straight past Jack and land on Clark. They would eat him alive.

'No, it's good having someone to ride with!' Jack yelled back.

Clark nearly fell off his bike in surprise.

'I'm going to stop for a picnic now. You can share if you like!' shouted Jack.

He started slowing down. Clark slowed down too. They pulled off into a passing-place on the narrow road.

The sky went dark as they took off their helmets. Black clouds covered the sun. But they weren't rain clouds – they were midges.

Whine! Buzz! They whizzed past Jack. They pounced on Clark.

He tried to brush them away. More and

more of them landed on him. He fell on
the ground, twisting and squirming under a
black blanket of midges.

'Help!' he yelled. 'Do something!'

Jack did something. He jumped back
on his motorbike and sped away! He had
the road to himself again. He felt happy

and free. He rode like the wind. And then suddenly he saw it – the sea.

He stopped on the cliff-top road and looked down across the waves.

'I did it!' he thought. 'I did it! What an amazing adventure that was!'

· CHAPTER 5 ·

'Have you seen Clark?' Mrs Merridew asked.

Jack shook his head. He climbed down off the motorbike.

'He's supposed to have swept around the cars on the forecourt, but it still looks messy to me,' Mrs Merridew grumbled. 'If you see him, can you tell him to come to the office?'

Jack nodded. She went back inside. He stayed there looking at the Bonneville. He was going to draw it for a poster so he

needed to remember exactly what it looked
like.

Uncle Archie came out of the workshop,
wiping his hands on his greasy boiler suit.
He strode across the yard.

'Have you seen Clark?' he asked.

Jack shook his head.

Uncle Archie frowned. 'He's supposed to be sorting out the new spare parts that came in this morning,' he grumbled. 'He's only done three boxes.'

He looked both ways and peered between the cars, but he couldn't see Clark anywhere.

'I can't hang around here all day,' he said. 'I've got to talk to Mrs Merridew about some orders. If you see Clark, can you tell him to come to the office?'

Jack nodded again and went back to admiring the motorbike. It had so much bright shiny chrome – what a good job he had just bought a silver gel pen with last week's pocket money!

Dad was nearby, talking to a customer. He showed her a couple of cars. After she had gone, he came across to see Jack.

'Have you seen Clark?' he said.

Jack shook his head.

'I still haven't managed to find him and have a word about what happened earlier,' grumbled Dad. 'Anyway, I've got to see Mrs Merridew about our ad in the Weekly News. So if you see Clark, can you send him over to the office?'

'Everyone's looking for Clark,' thought Jack. 'They're all after him like midges. He has to keep moving or they'll pounce on him.'

'Ooh!' thought Jack, gleefully. 'That gives me an idea.'

Jack got back on to the motorbike. He

knew that sooner or later, Clark would
come over. He could never resist the
chance to tease Jack. It didn't
take long.

'You're back on that big old
bike, then, Flapjack,' said
Clark. 'Mind you don't
fall off again!'

Jack wanted to say
'Go away' and 'Leave
me alone' but his plan
meant he had to be nice.

'You're right,' he said. 'It is a bit big.'
He got off again. Clark looked confused.
He didn't want Jack to agree with him. He
wanted Jack to get in a flap. Then he could
laugh and say, 'Don't get in a flap, Jack.
Flapjack! Get it?'

Jack said, 'Mrs Merridew's brought some home-made chocolate fudge cake today. She said we can go and get some from the office.'

Clark fell for it! He went across to the office with Jack. The minute he walked in

the door, they all pounced on him.

'When are you going to finish sweeping the forecourt?' demanded Mrs Merridew.

'When are you going to finish sorting out those boxes?' demanded Uncle Archie.

'I want a word with you,' said Dad.

Jack slipped past into the showroom. He got out his paper and pencils, and his new silver gel pen. He knew that Mrs Merridew, Uncle Archie and Dad wouldn't let Clark run away again. That meant he would have the rest of the morning to sit and draw in peace.

It was hard to draw a motorbike. It took a few tries to get the shape right. But after that came the best bit – the colouring-in. Jack did the blue tank, and then the black seat, tyres and handle-grips. Finally, he did the silver pipes and spirals. It looked brilliant.

Underneath he wrote:

Triumph Bonneville. It has a big beefy engine. Perfect for going on an adventure.

He showed his poster to Dad.

'Shall we pin it up on my Wall of Cars?' he asked. 'Do you think the customers will like it?'

Dad said he thought the customers

would love it – but the Bonneville wasn't for the customers.

'We don't sell motorbikes at the car supermarket,' he told Jack. 'And this one is not for sale.'

'Not for sale?' said Jack, in surprise.

Just then, a biker strode into the showroom. He was wearing black boots with lots of buckles and a leather jacket with fringes down the sleeves. He had his crash helmet under his arm.

'Where's my new motorbike, then?' he said.

'Grandpa?!' gasped Jack.

'Hello, my boy,' said Grandpa. 'Your dad has just sent me a text to say he's found a motorbike for me.'

'For you?' Jack exclaimed.

Grandpa nodded. 'Yes. I asked him to find one. I'm going to stop working at the bank soon and I wanted to buy myself a lovely leaving present!'

Jack thought the Bonneville would be the best leaving present in the world.

Grandpa leaned over to look at his poster.

'Is that my bike?' he asked. Jack nodded.

'What a great picture!' said Grandpa.

'You can have it if you like,' said Jack.

'We don't need it for the Wall of Cars.'

Grandpa looked delighted.

'I'll put it on my desk at the bank. Then

if I'm having a bad week, I can look at it
and think of all the adventures I'm going
to have when I leave.'

'That's what I do,' said Jack. 'If I'm
having a bad week, I think of all the
adventures I'm going to have in the cars on
Saturday morning.'

Times-tables tests, three-day-grumps,
puddles-and-poos, moaning Mum – none
of that mattered. For Car-mad Jack the
only thing that really mattered was cars.
And motorbikes, of course!

Look out for more of Car-mad Jack's adventures in the following books:

The Speedy Sports Car
The Versatile Van
The Marvellous Minibus
The Taxi About Town
The Rugged Off-roader